Myth Quest

Garuda

DEVOURER OF SERPENTS

retold by Anu Kumar

illustrations by Pen2Print Media Solutions

First published in 2011 by Hachette India
(Registered name: Hachette Book Publishing India Pvt. Ltd)
An Hachette UK company
www.hachetteindia.com

SRD

ISBN 978-93-5009-299-6

Hachette Book Publishing India Pvt. Ltd
612/614 (6th Floor), Time Tower,
M.G. Road, Sector 28, Gurgaon 122001, India

Typeset in Adobe Garamond Pro 13/16
by Eleven Arts, New Delhi

Printed and bound in India by
Manipal Technologies Limited, Manipal

Welcome to the world of MythQuest . . .

Discover the fables and legends about the origin, history, deities, ancestors and heroes of India.

While the term 'myth' in common conversation means a false story, in the world of religion, folklore and magic, myths are considered 'true'. They tell stories of the creation of the universe, the eternal battle between good and evil, and the history of humankind itself.

The main characters in our myths are bigger and better than any modern superheroes. They are birds and beasts, gods and demons, kings and queens, generals and warriors, sages and gurus, each with extraordinary powers that changed the course of history and the fate of the human race.

The people to whom a myth belongs consider it a true account of their past millions of years ago. Even today, they continue to worship the gods and goddesses, follow the rituals and read the texts that developed from these myths.

Hachette India's MythQuest series brings to you fascinating stories from the vast treasures of ancient mythology. Read them all—and become a MythMaster!

Mythological characters and events have been described in different ways in different versions of ancient texts. We have chosen the most interesting and key stories to build a comprehensive account for the young reader.

This book is about . . .

. . . Garuda, the magnificent half-man and half-bird who was the vahana *or mount of Vishnu, the Preserver of the Universe.*

Garuda, the guardian of Shiva's abode, is likened to a Brahminy kite and is also the Indian name for the Aquila constellation, which is patterned like an eagle. Garuda has been mentioned in the Rig Veda and the Mahabharata. He also has a whole Upanishad dedicated to him—the Garudopanishad. *The Garuda Purana, on the other hand, is a manual of instruction narrated to the bird-king by Lord Vishnu.*

In Buddhist mythology, Garuda is also known as Suparna and a vehicle of Amogasiddhi, a personification of the Buddhist quality of wisdom. He also features in the Kakati Jataka and Sussondi Jataka, among others.

Garuda is often represented as a creature with the head of a kite or an eagle, and the golden body and limbs of a man. It is said that his huge red wings billowed out as he flew across the sky and sounded like thunder. He could create hurricanes in the sky by merely flapping his wings.

Garuda is known by many names in different countries across the world and is the national emblem of Thailand and Indonesia. He is also the symbol of strength, speed and fighting skill as well as an avowed enemy of serpents.

Here are Garuda's quests, battles and victories set high among the clouds . . .

CHAPTER ONE

A TALE OF TWO EGGS

A very long time ago, there was a god called Daksha, who was the son of Brahma and Aditi. He was one of ancient *prajapatis,* or king of all creatures. He ruled over a kingdom somewhere between Heaven and earth. Daksha had many daughters, thirteen of whom were married to the holy sage, Kashyapa.

Two of the sage's wives, Vinata and Kadru, once used to be as close as sisters, but later they became rivals for their husband's affection.

Both Vinata and Kadru prayed to the gods for children. While Kadru wanted hundreds of them, Vinata prayed for a few powerful and gifted offspring. Finally, the gods, pleased with their devotion, granted both of them their wishes.

Kadru birthed a thousand eggs, which hatched into a thousand *nagas*, or snakes and serpents, and she became the mother of all the *nagas* of the world. Vinata, on the other hand, had only two eggs and they showed no sign of hatching for a long time. The gods told her to be patient, for her eggs would hatch only when they were ready. Five hundred years passed and the eggs remained intact, and Vinata grew more and more impatient. Finally, when she could hold back no longer, she broke one of them open.

Out of the egg came Aruna, her first son. But as he had emerged before time, he was born with

First published in 2011 by Hachette India
(Registered name: Hachette Book Publishing India Pvt. Ltd)
An Hachette UK company
www.hachetteindia.com

SRD

ISBN 978-93-5009-299-6

Hachette Book Publishing India Pvt. Ltd
612/614 (6th Floor), Time Tower,
M.G. Road, Sector 28, Gurgaon 122001, India

Typeset in Adobe Garamond Pro 13/16
by Eleven Arts, New Delhi

Printed and bound in India by
Manipal Technologies Limited, Manipal

CHAPTER TWO

A LIFE OF SLAVERY

Soon after Garuda was born, there took place a great war between the *asuras* and the *devas*, or the gods. At the end of it, both sides decided to strike a compromise and together they decided to undertake the *samudra manthan*, or churning of the Ocean of Milk, in order to find *amrita*, or the elixir of immortality. They used the Mount Mandara around which the serpent king Vasuki was wound, to stir up a storm in the ocean waters. This churning of the ocean yielded many offerings including several precious jewels, Airavata—the white elephant of the clouds, Uchchaishravas—the seven-headed divine horse as well as the deadly poison Halahala, which Lord Shiva swallowed and held in his throat. At last, the Physician of the Gods, Dhanvantari, emerged from the ocean, holding the pitcher containing the *amrita*.

Both Vinata and Kadru were also present during the *samudra manthan* and the moment they saw the beautiful horse, Uchchaishravas, break free of the ocean's foam, they could not take their eyes off him. 'What a beautiful horse!' said Vinata to her sister. 'Its colour is whiter than the snow on the high mountains.'

The wily Kadru decided to play a trick on her sister as she was extremely jealous of her and this was the perfect chance to trap her. 'Are you crazy?' she said, laughing scornfully. 'The horse looks quite black to me.'

Vinata thought her sister had become colour-blind and tried to convince her that the divine horse was indeed milk-white. Kadru, however, refused to listen. Then, she laid a bet with Vinata, saying that she

would prove her wrong. 'Oh come, Vinata, it's just a silly wager,' said Kadru with a false smile. 'Remember how we used to bet as children and then whoever lost would do the other's chores for the day. Only now, since we are older, the stakes should also be higher. So whoever loses will become the other one's slave for life.'

Vinata thought this was a friendly bet and she was sure of what she had seen, so she agreed. Her devious sister set her evil plot in motion. She summoned her thousand snake children and said, 'I want all of you who are completely black to cover every inch of that horse so that it looks like the colour of night. Thus Vinata will be proven wrong and will become my slave for life.'

The *nagas* did exactly as ordered. The black ones swam across the ocean waters and wriggled and crawled all over the horse, till not a single patch of white was visible.

Kadru took Vinata to the shore and pointed to the horse. 'See, the horse is black and so there—I have won the bet,' she said triumphantly. To her horror, Vinata saw the horse was indeed blacker than a moonless night and realized that she had been tricked.

This was no harmless wager and Aruna's curse had finally come true. So Vinata became Kadru's slave and had to live in the dark nether regions of the world, called *patala*, far away from her husband. Here, Vinata lived a cursed existence, guarded by hundreds of serpents who commanded her to do their foul and menial tasks.

CHAPTER THREE

GARUDA MEETS VISHNU

By this time, Garuda had emerged from the egg, splendid in form and divine in spirit. The moment he was born he saw how pathetic his mother's life was and how unbearable it was being a slave. Vinata had guarded her egg carefully after the fiasco with Aruna, and had taken it with her to *patala* and hidden it there in a safe place. However, when Garuda was born, he found himself at the mercy of the *nagas* and a slave to Kadru's whims.

Garuda was very proud and had no intention of following the orders of the *nagas*. Very soon, he realized

it was time he rescued his mother and freed himself from slavery. His mother blessed him and prayed that he would be successful. 'The wind shall protect your wings,' she said, 'the Moon shall protect your back, fire shall protect your head and the Sun will guard your whole body. And I shall always pray for your welfare.'

Garuda approached the serpents and asked them what it would take to purchase her freedom. They thought a while and then replied in unison. 'We want you to bring us the *amrita* that is being churned from the ocean's depths. Since the gods and *asuras* are both getting a part of it, we don't see why we should be missing a shot at immortality. Bring it to us and we will set you and your mother free,' they concluded with many loud hisses.

Now this was an order even the greatest of gods would have found difficult to obey. Once the *amrita* had been found, the gods had no more use for the *asuras* and certainly had no intention of sharing it with them. However, they did not want an outright confrontation and decided to fool them instead. Lord Vishnu took on the form of the beautiful *apsara,* or divine nymph, Mohini, and appeared on the banks of the ocean. She confounded the *asuras* with her beauty and while they sat enthralled, staring at her in a daze, she took the urn containing the *amrita* and vanished.

The urn with the *amrita* was kept in temple. It was surrounded by a massive everlasting fire whose flames reached high up into the sky, and was continuously fanned by strong winds. The way to the urn was blocked by a rotating door fixed with sharp blades. As a last hurdle, the gods had also stationed two hulking and poisonous snakes as the guardians of the urn.

However, Garuda was fearless and he hastened towards Heaven.

Aware of his intentions, and watching his threatening progress across the sky, the gods met him, clad in full battle armour. However, Garuda lashed out with his mighty wings and powerful talons—and the divine army was forced to retreat. He then effortlessly routed them by breathing fire, and then continued on his way to the temple.

Taking in the water of many sacred rivers into his

mouth, Garuda blew out the protective fire around the urn. Then reducing his size, he sneaked past the revolving door with its blades and spikes that would have cut up a larger creature in no time. Finally, when he encountered the two dangerous snake guardians, he flapped his wings quickly and blew dust into their eyes. Then, he used his sharp beak and mangled the blinded snakes to pieces in no time.

Garuda's flight to Heaven lasted twelve divine days, which equal twelve years of human time. Once he had got the *amrita*, Garuda held the elixir in his mouth carefully, without swallowing any of it. Then he headed back towards the eagerly waiting serpents.

On his way back, he encountered Lord Vishnu. The god had not come to fight Garuda. Instead, impressed by his speed, strength and presence of mind, Vishnu requested Garuda to become his *vahana*, or vehicle.

Garuda was flattered by the God's request, but he had two conditions. First, he wanted to be placed higher than the god himself in the order of worship by mortals and gods. Second, he desired the boon of immortality without drinking *amrita*.

Vishnu granted him both wishes. Thus was born the Garudadhvaja or the flag of Vishnu with Garuda adorning the top. Similarly, the Garudagamba or pillar found in front of Vishnu temples acquired a Garuda emblem at the pinnacle. From then on, devotees first got a glimpse of Garuda and then saw Vishnu.

There is another story about how Garuda became Vishnu's mount. One day Garuda was terribly hungry. On seeing that his appetite would not be easily satisfied, Vinata sent him to his father, Kashyapa.

Kashyapa told him that he could feed on the tribe of fishermen called the Nishadas. 'However, there is a Brahmin who lives in hiding among the Nishadas and you must not harm him in any way,' warned Kashyapa.

So Garuda went to the ocean shore and devoured the entire tribe of Nishadas. But as he did so, he accidentally swallowed the Brahmin as well and not knowing what to do, he returned to his father to ask for his advice.

Kashyapa spoke to the Brahmin who was still alive inside Garuda's stomach and offered to bring him out. However, this man was adamant. He insisted he would not come out unless the Nishadas were released too, as they had been his friends. Thus, Garuda had no option but to spit out everyone he had swallowed. That done, his stomach was empty again. The great bird-king was growing hungrier and weaker every moment.

Kashyapa came up with a new plan. He told Garuda about two brothers who had a long-lasting feud against each other. They had cursed each other and thus transformed into a mighty elephant and tortoise respectively. Despite changing into beasts, they continued to fight fiercely in the depths of the great ocean. 'They will make a good meal for you,' Kashyapa advised. 'Eat them and bring an end to their ridiculous war as well.'

Garuda set off. Soon, he found the two creatures and picked them up with his sharp talons and flew around looking for a place where he could devour them at leisure. But he soon found that no mountain or tree was strong enough to hold himself and his meal.

Finally, after flying for long, he saw a giant rose-apple tree and felt that it would be able to carry his weight. However, the moment he alighted on the tree, its branch broke into two.

Vishnu was watching all of this from Heaven and he felt pity for this great creature who was by now famished and tired of flying across the skies. He offered Garuda his own arm as a perch to sit and eat in peace. After the great bird had finished off his meal, he was still not sated and the benevolent Vishnu now offered him the flesh off his own arm. Garuda ate to his heart's content, and yet, not a wound appeared on Vishnu's arm.

At long last, Garuda had his fill and bowed low before Vishnu as he was humbled by the God's kindness. He offered himself to the god and asked if he could be of any help to him.

'I would like you to be my mount and carry me on

your majestic shoulders,' said Vishnu with a smile. 'You are the fastest and strongest creature in the skies and you would help me immensely in my long journeys across the universe.'

The bird-king gladly accepted the offer and from then onwards, he carried Vishnu on his journeys, quests and battles to ensure the preservation of the universe.

CHAPTER FOUR

A JUST COMPROMISE

After meeting Vishnu, Garuda once again resumed his journey to *patala* to free his mother from the *nagas*. However, the gods chased him, determined to retrieve the precious *amrita*. Indra, the King of Heaven even attacked him with his thunderbolt, Vajra, but Garuda was far too strong and quick even for Indra and continued unscathed on his journey.

Indra, however, refused to give up and gave him chase. At last, a tired and irritated Garuda decided to reach some sort of a compromise with the God.

Garuda promised that once he had delivered the *amrita*, he would trick the snakes with a diversion, and

then Indra and the other gods would be able to regain possession of the precious nectar.

Indra, in turn, blessed Garuda with a boon. 'From today, you will rule over and feed on all the snakes and they will flee in terror at your sight,' he said raising his powerful thunderbolt to the sky.

When the serpents received the *amrita* from Garuda, they were overjoyed and at once released Vinata from her long years of enslavement. Although the snakes had fulfilled their promise to Garuda and released him and his mother, Indra's boon had made him an eternal enemy of the serpents.

The moment his mother was free, Garuda put his second plan into action. He spat the *amrita* he had held in his beak and throat onto the long spiky blades of the *kusha* grass that grew by the bank of the river that the snakes bathed in. He told the snakes that they could come and lick it up from the blades of grass after their purification bath. As the snakes frolicked in the water, little did they know that Garuda had hatched a devious plan to fool them.

Hidden from the *nagas*, Indra quietly appeared and quickly collected all the nectar from the *kusha* grass and returned with it to Heaven.

When the snakes emerged from the water, they slithered eagerly to the *kusha* grass to lick up the precious *amrita*. However, it was in vain, as every last drop of it had been taken by Indra. The snakes licked each blade furiously, searching for the *amrita* that would make them immortal and ignoring the sharp blades of the *kusha* grass—so sharp that it slit their tongues into two. After a long, long time they realized that there was no *amrita* and all they had for their efforts was a permanently forked tongue. Not only this, but every snake that was born thereafter had a forked tongue.

The *kusha* grass on the other hand, had been touched by the *amrita*, even if it were for a short while and was forever regarded as a sacred plant associated with the gods.

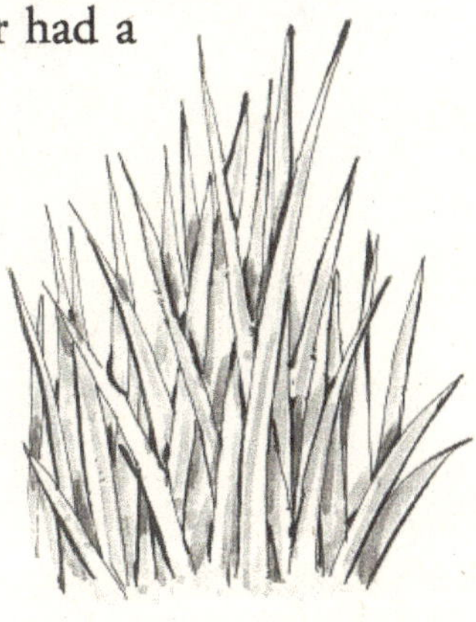

CHAPTER FIVE

THE FOLLY OF ARROGANCE

Garuda was a proud creature. He enjoyed his power as Vishnu's mount and his elevated position on the Garudadhvaja and the Garudagamba. He also revelled in his power as the Devourer of Snakes, a name that had stuck ever since he had been blessed by Indra's boon. Every single snake in the world would tremble with fear at the mere mention of Garuda's name.

However, there was one snake who did not fear Garuda. His name was Maninaga and he had pleased

Shiva with his great devotion. As a result he had been granted a great boon that protected him from Garuda. He wandered around freely everywhere and did not run away even when he was face to face with the bird-king.

This irritated Garuda and he captured Maninaga in order to teach him a lesson. Since he could not kill him, he kept the snake imprisoned and treated him very badly indeed.

Now Shiva's *vahana* Nandi came to know of this and informed his master about his devotee's misfortune. Shiva did not want to get involved in a tussle with Vishnu's *vahana* and so he advised Nandi to tackle this matter diplomatically. 'Go offer your prayers to the great Preserver of the Universe. This will please him immensely as you are the divine bull, after all. Once he is pleased with your devotion, he will grant you any wish,' concluded the great Three-eyed One.

Nandi immediately started praying to Vishnu and sure enough, the god was flattered with the attention from Shiva's favourite *gana*, or follower and appeared before the bull.

'What is it that you desire, O Divine Bull?' asked the Preserver of the Universe.

'I have only one desire,' said Nandi, folding his hands. 'Please allow Maninaga to be freed from Garuda's clutches.' Vishnu knew he might offend Garuda. Yet, he

could not refuse to grant Nandi's wish. So he blessed the bull and asked Garuda to release the snake.

Garuda did as he was told, although he was not pleased with the turn of events. 'Lord, this is unfair,' he protested. 'Other masters are so considerate towards their followers, whereas you never ever praise me,' he complained. 'Now when I have finally got something through my own efforts, you ask me to return it. I don't think this is fair. You ride on my back whenever you need to go to battle and I take you there faster than light. In fact, I think you defeat all your enemies because of my skills alone.'

Vishnu waited till Garuda had finished speaking and then he responded to his surly complaints with a smile. 'Garuda, you are right. You have indeed borne my weight all these years and it is true that I have been victorious because of your great strength alone. Maybe you should not carry all of me. I will make it easier for you and from now, all you need to do, is just bear the weight of my little finger.'

Saying this, Vishnu placed his little finger on Garuda's head. The mighty god's finger was so heavy that the great Garuda fell to the ground under its pressure. He suddenly lost all his great strength and felt as weak as a newborn fledgling.

He at once realized the folly of his arrogance and the great power that Vishnu wielded.

'Please forgive me, O Lord,' he pleaded. 'I have been suitably punished for my false pride by being squashed by your little finger alone. Master, help me recover my lost strength again for I have learnt my lesson,' said Garuda meekly.

Maninaga was freed from captivity. Vishnu then asked Nandi to take Garuda to Lord Shiva's abode at Mount Kailash, for only Lord Shiva had the power that would undo Vishnu's punishment and restore Garuda to his former might. Shiva told Garuda to bathe in the holy Ganga river. The bird-king followed the god's instructions and took several dips in the sacred waters. Each time he emerged, a little bit of his old strength returned. Finally, after many immersions, Garuda came out resplendent in his renewed strength and glory.

CHAPTER SIX

GARUDA SAVES THE DAY

The same Ganga that revived Garuda had not always flowed across earth, giving life to the land and its people with her holy waters. This was a time when the earth had run dry as a result of the strife between the gods and the *asuras*. Finally, after many years, Ganga was brought down from Heaven by a great prince of Ayodhya.

The story begins with King Sagara of the Ikshvaku dynasty. This great ancestor of Rama once decided to hold a Ashwamedha Yagna, or the great horse sacrifice. Fearing the power that Sagara would gain through this

sacrifice, Indra stole the sacred horse for the *yagna* and left it with sage Kapila for safekeeping. Sagara sent all his sixty thousand sons to look for the horse and they reached the hermitage of the great sage.

However, in the process they disturbed his meditation and all of them were charred to death by Kapila's fiery gaze.

As the royal princes had died an ignoble death, their souls found no release and wandered the earth as shadows. They needed to be propitiated with holy water or they would be forever doomed. However, no one could find any holy water for the ablutions.

Many years later, his grandson Anshuman was sent to Kapila as an emissary of peace. While Kapila returned the sacred horse to Anshuman, there was still no peace for Sagara's hapless deceased sons.

Anshuman was distressed for he did not know how to obtain the water to purify the dead. This was a bad portent for the whole dynasty, which would never prosper if the souls of its ancestors were not at peace.

He sat weeping in a forest when Garuda flew right over him. As he chanced upon the sobbing man, he immediately swooped down to see what the matter was. Upon hearing Anshuman's predicament, he thought deeply for a while.

Now Garuda had the wisdom and foresight of the gods themselves and he prophesied that Anshuman's forefathers would soon be saved by another brave son of the dynasty. 'He will be the one to induce Ganga to descend from Heaven,' Garuda announced, 'and she will save all the souls of the dead with her flowing waters.'

Garuda's prophecy was fulfilled by Anshuman's grandson, Bhagirath, who finally persuaded Ganga to come down to earth and so freed his dynasty from the curse.

Garuda continued to be associated with the Ikshvaku dynasty and rendered great service to many of its kings including Prince Rama, the greatest king of the dynasty and an avatar of Lord Vishnu himself. Garuda joined Rama's forces in the battle against Ravana at a crucial moment in the war when things looked very gloomy for the Ayodhya prince.

One of Ravana's finest warriors was his son Meghnad who had even defeated Indra in battle. He was a great devotee of Lord Shiva and had spent many years praying to him. Lord Shiva had been pleased with his devotion and given him valuable knowledge of many weapons, all of which he now set out to employ in the battle against Rama.

He unleashed the magical arrow called the *nagapaash* or the serpent noose, which released a large coiled snake that wrapped itself around both Rama and Laksmana, making it difficult for them to even move, let alone fight back. It also let out several fiery serpents as arrows that struck the brothers and rendered them unconscious. The *vanara* or monkey army watched helplessly as their leaders lay lifelessly on the ground.

It was at this moment of great despondency that Garuda appeared in the skies.

He appeared in a blaze of thunder and lightning, and lit up the whole sky. The wind blew louder, the mountains shook violently and the ocean waves rose high in terrible warning. The *vanara* army looked on awestruck as Garuda approached the battlefield, flapping his immense red wings. Ravana's army began to scatter and flee in fear. Every snake that had been released from the *nagapash* quickly scuttled away at the mere sight of him. The wind blew stronger and a huge trail of fire followed the great bird-king. The mountains shook violently and the ocean waves surged high.

As Garuda's fiery breath scorched the very air, the huge snake that bound Rama and Laksmana quickly uncoiled and disappeared into a burrow in the earth for there was no *naga* on this earth that could face this all-powerful devourer of snakes.

When Garuda finally landed on earth, all the snakes let loose by the *nagapaash* had disappeared. However, Rama and Lakshmana had fallen unconscious under the attack of this powerful weapon.

Once again Garuda came to the rescue. He leaned over Rama and Lakshmana, and gently waved his wings over them, fanning the princes back to life with his magic powers.

Soon, Rama and Laksmana awoke from their trance. They recovered from their wounds rapidly and resumed the fight, but not before Rama had thanked the great Garuda.

'Dear Garuda, you have saved us as well as this war against evil,' said Rama, clasping Garuda's giant arm in gratitude. 'I will never forget this favour that you have rendered us. From today, you will be like a brother to me.' And this eternal friendship continued through Rama's life as well as his other avatars, for Rama was only one of the divine Vishnu's many incarnations. And Garuda continued to serve his Lord whenever Vishnu required his assistance in his various divine and human avatars and fought by his side in all his battles against injustice and terror.

CHAPTER SEVEN

A BATTLE AND A BOON

Garuda had helped Vishnu in his avatar as Rama—in the same way, he was at his Lord's side when Vishnu appeared as Krishna, and accompanied him on his various battles against the evil *asuras*. One such battle was against Narakasura, an evil demon king, who ruled over the kingdom of Pragjyotishpur.

Infamous for his wicked ways, Narakasura had defeated Indra in battle. His cruelty knew no bounds and he had plagued gods and humans alike. Indra, the Lord of Heaven, requested Krishna to

kill the demon and thus free Heaven and earth from his tyranny.

Krishna agreed, and along with his wife Satyabhama and Garuda, flew towards Pragjyotishpur, Narakasura's kingdom. Pragjyotishpur was a well-fortified city constructed by the five-headed demon Mura. There was a formidable fort in each of the four directions and it was protected on all sides by a huge army of *asuras*. There was also a canal all around the kingdom as well as an invisible barrier composed of *anila*, a poisonous gas. There was also an unbreakable barbed-wire fence that stood like an impregnable wall all around the kingdom.

Refusing to be daunted by such obstacles, Krishna shattered the forts to pieces with one blow of his mace. Mura, who lived underwater, awoke from his deep sleep at the deafening sound of the ramparts collapsing. He burst forth from the waters, looking as fierce as the blazing midday sun. He took one furious look what had happened, took aim and then let his trident fly at Garuda.

Krishna was prepared for all of Mura's moves. The demon's fiery countenance made all other beings turn away from him, but had no effect on Krishna. As the trident moved in a wide arc towards Garuda, he let loose two arrows from his own quiver and they broke Mura's trident into pieces.

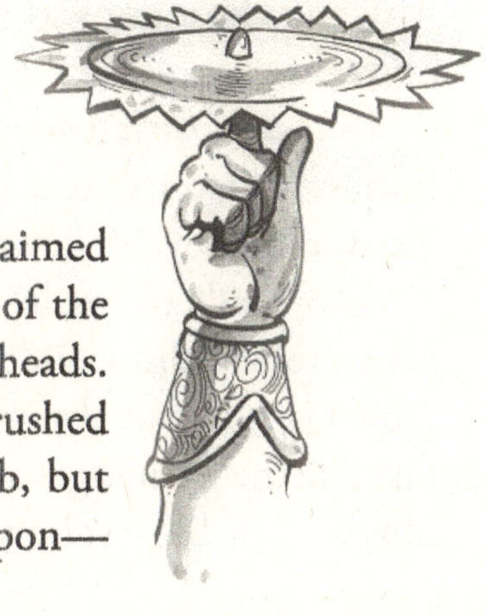

Then with a flurry of well-aimed arrows, Krishna pierced each of the mouths on the demon's five heads. Thoroughly enraged, Mura rushed towards Krishna with his club, but Krishna, using his divine weapon—

the Sudarshan Chakra—killed him with a single blow. A terrible battle then ensued between Krishna and Narakasura.

Meanwhile, the demon king's army of *asuras* had to deal with Garuda. The great bird-king alone was enough for the whole army of *asuras*. He effortlessly wiped out rank after rank of demon warriors by first stunning them by breathing fire and smoke. Then he destroyed them completely by gouging their eyes with his strong beak. All the *asuras* in Narakasura's army dropped to the ground under Garuda's assault.

This divine warrior wrought such complete destruction that there was not a single demon or beast standing alive apart from Narakasura himself who was the strongest among the *asuras*. He hurled a weapon granted him by the goddess Shakti towards Krishna. This was immediately deflected by Krishna's wife Satyabhama. When Krishna saw his wife's hand bleeding with the effort, he was furious and smote the mighty *asura* down with his Sudarshan Chakra.

Thus the battle ended and once again Garuda had fulfilled his duty as a great *vahana*, an unmatched warrior and loyal follower of Lord Vishnu.

As a result of his loyal service, Garuda received a boon from Vishnu, which was in the form of a Purana. Now Garuda had always wished to compose a Purana just like the great sages and having a Purana named for him was the biggest honour for the bird-king. He first

recited it to his father, Kashyapa. Then, Vishnu himself recited the Garuda Purana to the other gods. Ved Vyasa, the ancient sage who composed the Mahabharata, learnt the Purana from Brahma and taught it to his disciples. Apart from being an instruction manual on astronomy, medicine, grammar and gemstones, this Purana also described Vishnu in all his manifestations from Matsya to Kalki.

The Garuda Purana was forever after proof that this great bird-king was not merely a symbol of strength but also a repository of generations of wisdom.

CHAPTER EIGHT

THE STORY OF A LITTLE BIRD

This great king of birds was also a creature of deep compassion. Garuda was a benevolent monarch who had great love for all his bird subjects no matter how insignificant they were in the order of the universe.

Once, perched on Mount Kailash, the abode of the god Shiva, Garuda noticed a tiny bird hopping around. Just then, Yama, the God of Death appeared, riding his black buffalo. Garuda noticed that Yama looked at the bird for a brief moment before he continued on his way to meet Shiva.

Garuda knew that a mere glance from Lord Yama could mean death and his heart was filled with pity for the tiny creature. He gently picked it up and clutched it tenderly in his powerful talons. Then Garuda took the bird and flew far away till he reached a deep forest. There, he placed the tiny bird on a rock beside a running stream. Then, he returned to Mount Kailash and assumed his earlier position on the mountain as one of its guardians.

When Yama emerged from his meeting with Shiva, he greeted Garuda in a friendly manner. Garuda stopped him as he was going out and said, 'Just before you went in, I saw you looking at a little bird. You had a very sad expression on your face. May I know why?' he asked.

'When my eyes fell on the bird, I saw that very soon it would meet its death in the jaws of a huge python and thus I was saddened,' answered Yama. 'But in Kailash, there are no serpents, and thus I was wondering how this would happen.'

Garuda stood still in shock as he realized that he had just delivered the little creature to its death despite his best efforts.

A tear rolled down his cheek at the fate of his little subject. He was sad, but he also became aware of the undeniable power of destiny, which controlled the great and the small alike.

CHAPTER NINE

GREAT SNAKES

The great bird-king Garuda was wise and benevolent—and not just to his subjects alone. He extended his kindness even to his worst enemies—the *nagas*.

The island of Ramanaka-dvipa had the largest number of snakes in the universe. Following the advice of Brahma, Creator of the Universe, all the *nagas* of the island came to pay obeisance to Garuda.

'O mighty king,' they said, 'our race will never survive if you eat us all.' Garuda respected the general order of the universe, which in turn depended on the continuation of all the species in it. He agreed to spare the snakes and in return, the grateful *nagas* arranged a monthly sacrificial offering from their side.

This arrangement worked well until one month, things went terribly wrong. Kaliya, a monstrous, many-headed serpent arrived at the *naga* temple and ate up the snake kept there as an offering for Garuda. The bird-king arrived at his usual spot looking forward to his regular offering. However, this month the altar was empty!

Garuda was livid because he thought the snakes had broken the promise. The snakes told the king of birds how they had left an offering as usual and how it had been eaten by the evil Kaliya despite their warnings and pleas.

On hearing this, Garuda grew furious. He hunted Kaliya down and then gave this giant serpent such a violent kick that he fell to the ground unconscious.

However, Kaliya was no ordinary serpent and he quickly recovered from the blow and reared up his many

heads and hissed menacingly at Garuda. The king of birds flew at him, attacking him with his sharp beak and muscular arms, while Kaliya sat up erect, spitting venom from his many tongues.

The fight was fierce. Kaliya swelled in size till he towered over the bird-king. Garuda too assumed his divine form. He grabbed Kaliya in his immense talons and threw him to the ground. He then beat him with his wings, over and over until Kaliya lay completely stunned.

At last, Kaliya, unable to continue this fight, ran away. But Garuda refused to give up the chase and followed Kaliya across the universe. Realizing that no one except Lord Vishnu could save him, Kaliya finally reached the God's abode and fell at his feet, begging for mercy and protection.

Vishnu took mercy on Kaliya and told him to take shelter in the river Yamuna, since Garuda was forbidden from entering its holy waters due to a curse from the sage Saubhari. Garuda used to catch and eat the fish from the Yamuna. Now this was a river greatly loved by the sage as he meditated on its bank. He requested Garuda to leave the fish of this particular river alone. Although Garuda did not wish to disobey the revered sage, he just could not resist carrying off one last exceptionally large fish. When Saubhari came to know of this, he was enraged and he cursed Garuda, saying, 'If you ever come to this river again, you will die.'

Thus Kaliya took advantage of this curse and hid in

the river Yamuna without fear of Garuda. He continued with his evil ways, until he was defeated and killed by Krishna, one of the incarnations of Vishnu himself.

This was not the only great snake that Garuda battled. There was a time when he entered into a tussle with Vasuki, the great flying serpent.

Despite being a demon, Balasura was honourable and he sacrificed his body to the gods as they needed it for a holy fire. However, while the heavenly deities were travelling with the body, it fell from their divine *vimana*, or flying vehicle. As his body fell to the earth, it shattered into a million pieces. Each spot where a piece of Balasura's body fell magically transformed into a treasure trove of precious gems.

All the creatures of the world including the kings and the *devas* came forth to get a piece of Balasura's magical flesh. Among them was Vasuki. One of the most powerful *nagas* and as old as the universe itself, Vasuki was the great snake-king who could traverse any realm. In a flash, he reached the spot where Balasura's bile was falling to the earth. He opened his jaws wide and consumed all of the greenish yellow fluid that fell from the skies in a trice. He was flying back to *patala* when he was suddenly attacked by Garuda.

The bird-king had been watching Balasura's body fall from the skies and also wanted some of this unbelievable wealth that was suddenly appearing on different parts of earth. When he saw Vasuki drinking the bile, he

thought this was the perfect opportunity to steal the precious fluid as well as battle his archenemy.

As the two creatures fought, both Heaven and earth trembled. Finally, Garuda got an upper hand and managed to trap the great king of snakes in a stranglehold. Choking in the grasp of the mighty Garuda, Vasuki was forced to spit out the swallowed bile.

Garuda swooped down after it, but it fell to the earth before he could catch it, and immediately changed into *marakatas*, or emeralds.

As he watched the green precious stones glittering in the sunlight, Garuda thought that earth was a better place for them. He also realized that the lust for such material wealth often ended badly. He made peace with Vasuki and flew back to his heavenly abode.

MythNotes

A legend from south India recounts how a devotee of Vishnu once carved an image of Garuda out of wood, which then came to life and flew into the air. At the Parakkai village in Tamil Nadu, an artisan unknowingly hurled his chisel at Garuda, injuring his right wing. Garuda fell to earth crying out Vishnu's name repeatedly. A four-armed image of Vishnu was later installed on the very spot that Garuda fell.

As Garuda is a symbol of speed and the king of the skies, it is perhaps fitting that the national airline of Indonesia is known as Garuda. In India, there is a special branch of the Indian Air Force, called Garud Commando Force, which specializes in complex war operations.

The famous Balinese dancers often wear Garuda masks and enact stories from the bird-king's life.

Garuda is believed to have lived on an island called Salmalidvipa which was surrounded on all sides by the Sura Sea, or sea of wine. Salmalidvipa had seven mountain ranges, rich in precious gems and medicinal herbs. It also had seven rivers whose waters washed away all sins.

In Buddhist texts, Garuda is the king of the class of beings who are half-bird and half-god, known as suparnas. *It is this Buddhist representation of Garuda that is commonly seen in Japan, Indonesia, Mongolia, Thailand and other parts of Asia. The worship of Garuda as well as the presence of this great creature as an iconic symbol in religion, art and mythology is seen across many cultures and countries.*